Junkyard Dan

Money for Nothing

NOX PRESS

books for that extra kick to give you more power
www.NoxPress.com

Also by Elise Leonard:

The **JUNKYARD DAN** series: (***Nox Press***)
1. Start of a New Dan
2. Dried Blood
3. Stolen?
4. Gun in the Back
5. Plans
6. Money for Nothing
7. Stuffed Animal
8. Poison, Anyone?
9. A Picture Tells a Thousand Dollars
10. Wrapped Up
11. Finished
12. Bloody Knife
13. Taking Names and Kicking Assets
14. Mercy

THE SMITH BROTHERS (a series): (***Nox Press***)
1. All for One
2. When in Rome
3. Get a Clue
4. The Hard Way
5. Master Plan

A LEEG OF HIS OWN (a series): (***Nox Press***)
1. Croaking Bullfrogs, Hidden Robbers
2. 20,000 LEEGS Under the C
3. Failure to Lunch
4. Hamlette

The **AL'S WORLD** series: (***Simon & Schuster***)
Book 1: Monday Morning Blitz
Book 2: Killer Lunch Lady
Book 3: Scared Stiff
Book 4: Monkey Business

The **LEADER** series: (***Nox Press***)
- ✯ Honor
- ✯ Courage
- ✯ Respect
- ✯ Service
- ✯ Integrity
- ✯ Commitment
- ✯ Loyalty
- ✯ Duty

Junkyard Dan

Money for Nothing

Elise Leonard

NOX PRESS
books for that extra kick to give you more power
www.NoxPress.com

Leonard, Elise
Junkyard Dan series / Money for Nothing
ISBN: 978-0-9815694-5-1

Copyright © 2008 by Elise Leonard.
All rights reserved, including the right of reproduction in whole or in part in any form. Published by Nox Press.
www.NoxPress.com

First Nox Press printing: June 2008
Second Nox Press printing: March 2009
Third Nox Press printing: April 2010

books for that extra kick to give you more power

As always, for my readers, my family, my friends.
And to some great new friends:
the folks and teachers at the
Biddeford Adult Education, Maine
First Teachers Family Literacy Program.
Particularly, Patty Hallczuk and Julie Berube.
Your praise and support, as well as your
determination to get more materials to your
learners was not only noted (and greatly
appreciated), but gave us the spirit and strength we
needed to get more books out there!

And isn't that *exactly*
what teachers are supposed to DO?!
Get people to give their all
through praise and encouragement?
Well, it worked! ☺
Money for Nothing is here thanks to
Patty and Julie. You are TRUE educators,
and your learners are lucky to have you!

You guys ROCK!

Many thanks to Greg and Gwen Pettit, the owners of the cool 1971 Ford Torino on the cover. The car has 900 HP, and goes from 0 to 60 in less than 2 seconds! Greg has owned the car since 1987. It's like a family member. So when Greg and Gwen got married in 1996, he made sure Gwen knew she was marrying them *both*! Good luck, Greg, while racing! Be safe and be *fast!*

~Elise

Chapter 1

The phone rang.

I answered it.

It was Bubba.

"So where *are* you?" he asked.

I rolled my eyes. "Didn't *you* call *me*?"

"Yes," he said.

"So where do you *think* I am?!"

"Oh. Right. At your desk," he said with a chuckle.

Now that we'd answered *that* question, he had another one.

"Why aren't you at the diner?" he asked.

I thought we'd answered that already.

"Because I'm at my desk."

"No," Bubba said. "I mean why aren't you at the funeral?"

"What funeral?"

"Jose's."

I'd known a couple of Joses. But they were all in New York.

And I doubted they were getting buried in Peaceville just for me.

"I didn't know your Jose," I stated.

"*That* doesn't matter," Bubba said.

"Look. Bubba. I'm not going to a man's funeral if I didn't know him," I exclaimed.

"You're in Peaceville now, Dan. We do things differently here."

I was about to argue.

Then I saw Miles. He was in a suit. And headed for my office.

He saw me through the screen door.

"Are you coming to the funeral? Or not?" Miles called to me.

"I don't know if I'm invited," I said.

Miles pulled the door open. He came in and

Money for Nothing

grinned.

"*Everyone's* invited. This is Peaceville!" he said.

"See?" Bubba said from the other end of the phone.

I rolled my eyes.

"I'm hanging up now," I told Bubba.

"Okay. But you're coming. Right?" he asked.

"I guess I am," I said.

Then I hung up.

I looked at Miles.

"You look good," I told him.

He shrugged. "It's a funeral."

"True. But you still look good," I said.

He shrugged. "I'm just glad it's not *my* funeral."

He didn't smile, but I knew he was joking.

"I'd be wearing the same suit, though," he added. "If it were."

Now he was smiling.

"'Cause I *know* I look good!" he said with humor.

He was a character.

He never said or did what I expected him to say or do.

That was one of the things I liked about him.

One of many.

"Are you going to wear that?" he asked me.

He was pointing to my jeans and t-shirt.

"I wasn't planning on going to a funeral today," I said. "I didn't even *know* Jose."

"Son," he said simply. "Let me tell you a little something. Okay?"

I shrugged. "Sure."

"I've been around a lot longer than you have."

That was true.

He was much older than I was.

"And I've got to tell you," he said strongly. "Funerals are for the living. Not for the dead."

He *was* older. And, as you can tell by what he'd just said? He was wiser, too.

"Plus, you would have liked Jose," Miles added.

"I'm sure I would have," I agreed.

"I'm not saying that because he's passed on," Miles said.

He looked me in the eye.

"I'm saying that because you *really* would have liked him."

I nodded.

"He was a leader of men," Miles said softly. "A man who had a passion. A man who did something positive with his life."

"What did he do?" I asked.

"He gave people power. He gave people strength. He gave people a voice."

Chapter 2

I was almost done getting dressed.

I was just tying my tie.

Miles was out feeding the dogs. And cats.

I could hear him talking to them.

"How are ya'll doing?" he asked them.

They didn't answer.

"Did you miss me?" he asked them.

Again, no answer.

"*I* missed *you*," he told them. "But I had places to go. People to see."

They still didn't respond.

But I wondered. Who did Miles go to see when he left here?

Where did he go?

Money for Nothing

He was a very private man.

I really knew little about him.

Other than some basic facts. Like, he was old.

I knew that.

And homeless.

I knew that as well.

I knew that I *liked* him.

So I guess that was enough to know.

What more did I need to know?

I knew enough to know I liked him.

I also respected him.

And with that respect, goes understanding. And acceptance.

If he wanted his privacy? I'd give him that. Out of respect.

The phone rang. It was Bubba again.

"Are you coming?" Bubba asked. "Or not?"

"Yes, I'm coming. So is Miles."

"I'm at the diner," Bubba said.

"We'll be there in a few minutes," I told him.

The drive to the diner was pleasant.

Elise Leonard

"Nice day for a funeral," Miles said softly.

I shrugged. "If *any* day is nice for a funeral."

"I hate when it's pouring rain. Or storming," he explained.

He looked out the front window as I drove.

"It's bad enough that you're grieving. It's hard enough that you're missing the person. But to have to go through bad weather? To say goodbye? It just doesn't seem right," he said.

He shook his head.

It seemed as if he'd been there before. A wet, stormy funeral.

I guess when you're saying goodbye to someone you love? It's easier if it's sunny. Or bright.

Saying goodbye is hard enough.

"You're right," I told Miles. "I've never thought about it before."

He didn't answer. Just sort of grunted a little.

We were near the diner.

"Wow," I said. "Look at all the cars on Main Street!"

Money for Nothing

"Everyone's at the diner," Miles said.

"I can see that," I said.

"That's where we always go," he explained. "Before *and* after the funerals."

I thought of Hilda.

I knew someone had died and all. But I couldn't help myself from thinking I was glad she was getting some business.

She was an amazing cook. And an even better person.

"I think I'll have to park way over here," I said.

I was looking for a closer spot. But today? There were none.

Usually I could park right out in front.

But not today.

Chapter 3

We were walking toward the diner.

"My goodness," I said to Miles. "I didn't know there were so many folks living in Peaceville."

"Oh," he said. He shook his head. "The people you will see today? They will come from *all* over."

"Jose was well known?" I asked.

"No. Well, maybe. Possibly. But it's the people that Jose helped who will be here today. So expect a huge crowd."

I was impressed.

"He helped that many people?" I asked.

Miles nodded.

"Was he wealthy?" I asked.

Money for Nothing

"In his own way," Miles said. His smile was warm.

It seemed like he was thinking about Jose. Remembering Jose.

I wanted to ask Miles what Jose did. How Jose had helped so many people. But I didn't want to intrude on his thoughts.

Miles was smiling widely.

We walked in silence to the diner.

I guess Bubba saw us through the window.

He came outside and started walking toward us.

"Man! Look at *you*!" he said.

Then he whistled.

Like he was whistling at a girl.

It was embarrassing.

But that's probably why he did it.

Bubba liked to stir things up.

"Danggit, Dan!" he said. He was staring at my suit. "Is that how you dressed for work every day?"

"It's how I *used* to dress."

"Man. That is one *fine* suit!" Bubba said. "And

you," he said to Miles.

Before he could say anything? Miles spoke.

"You don't have to tell me," Miles said. "I *know* I look sharp!"

"You're looking pretty good too," I told Bubba.

Bubba turned pink.

"Yeah?" he asked.

I smiled slightly.

"You look good," Miles told Bubba.

"I feel stupid in this," he said. His hands waived at the suit he was wearing.

"Well, you look good," I said again.

Bubba reached his hand under his collar.

"I feel like I'm choking," he said. "Like I'm wearing a dog collar. And it's too tight."

That was funny. But not for the reasons you'd think.

You see, *normally*? Bubba wore a leather collar around his neck. A black leather collar. It had silver studs on it. Looked mighty scary.

But *that* was an actual collar.

A *tie* was not an actual collar.

Money for Nothing

But I could see how he felt it was.

I used to think my tie felt like a collar. Every day. When I was a stock broker. In New York. On Wall Street.

But now? I don't have to wear a tie.

Just jeans and a t-shirt.

Every day. All day.

It was nice.

"So you're coming. Right?" Bubba asked me.

"Where?" I asked.

"To the *funeral*," he said. He looked like he was getting annoyed.

"What funeral?" I asked.

Bubba snorted a laugh.

"You're just playing with me now. Aren't you?" he said.

I tried not to smile. "Yup."

We'd reached the diner door.

Bubba pulled it open.

"Well, come on in. Everyone's here," Bubba said.

I stopped short.

Miles bumped into the back of me.

"I still feel funny," I said. "Going to a man's funeral when I didn't know him."

"I already *told* you," Bubba said with a huff. "That doesn't matter!"

"Of course it matters," I said back. "I just feel funny."

"Why?" Bubba asked.

I thought about that. "I don't know. I've never done it before," I said.

"Well, go on in the diner," Miles said.

He gave me a little push.

"You'll learn all you need to know about Jose," he added.

"And by the time we go to the *funeral*?" Bubba said. "You'll feel as if you've known Jose your whole life."

Chapter 4

The crowd was huge.

The place was packed.

People were all telling stories. And they were laughing out loud.

For a funeral? It seemed a bit festive.

Hilda was in her glory.

She was rushing around.

Getting people soda. And coffee.

And anything else they wanted.

She looked a little tired. But happy.

Very, *very* happy.

"Hi, Dan," she called from across the room.

I didn't want to shout back.

So I just waved.

She lifted an empty coffee cup.

It rocked on the saucer.

I was afraid it was going to fall off. And smash.

But Hilda made it settle down.

I should have known. She always has things under control.

"Coffee?" she called to me.

I still didn't want to shout. So I nodded.

I'd never turn down Hilda's coffee. Her coffee was amazing.

Mine? Not so good.

I never learned the art of making good coffee.

Sometimes? Bubba wouldn't drink my coffee.

Heck. There are times *I* wouldn't drink it!

I looked around. There were no tables.

Well, there *were* tables. But none empty.

It was standing room only.

"I see someone I know," Bubba said. "I'll be right back."

"Go ahead," I said.

"I'm going to the men's room," Miles said.

Then he left.

Money for Nothing

I was alone now. So I watched the people.

This crowd was more like what I was used to. In New York.

The only difference? The people here? They were all talking to each other.

In New York? They'd work very hard *not* to talk to each other.

You see. In New York? There are so many people? And it is *so* crowded? People need to ignore each other.

I know. That sounds weird.

But I guess you have to live there to know why.

When you can't get away from people? *Ever*? No matter where you go? Or when you go? You have to work at ignoring them.

It's the only way. If you want a little privacy.

It really *is* the city that never sleeps.

And I think all those people? They just walk around. And walk around. And don't go home!

Because in New York? You can *never* get away from people!

So we end up ignoring each other. To get our

space. Our privacy.

Sounds stupid. But it makes sense.

Here? In the diner? The large crowd was noisy.

It sounded like a freight train was passing through.

It sounded like thunder.

Thunder that didn't end.

I barely heard Hilda.

But I saw her.

And that was all I needed to forget the crowd.

In one hand? She had a cup of coffee. In the other? A plate of pie.

It looked like apple.

Did I mention? It was a la mode! You know. With ice cream on top.

Vanilla.

My favorite.

I hoped it was for me.

She headed right for me.

Yes. I think it *was* for me.

I hadn't asked for pie.

But then, I hadn't asked for coffee, either.

Money for Nothing

Hilda just knew.

Knew what I wanted.

She held out the cup and saucer to me.

My eyes only saw the pie.

Hilda laughed.

"You sure do love my pie!" she shouted.

It was noisy. And getting noisier. What a racket.

"Yes I do," I agreed.

"It's bare," she said.

"No it's not," I said.

"What?" she shouted.

"It's not bare," I shouted. "You put the ice cream on top."

"Not bare. *Bear*!" she screamed shrilly.

"Bear pie?" I'd heard of mincemeat pie. But I'd never heard of bear pie.

Although people *do* eat meat pies. Often.

Maybe someone went hunting or something.

I started to wonder. Does ice cream go well on bear pie?

It didn't seem like it would.

Chapter 5

I wasn't all that excited.

Not about bear pie.

But if Hilda made it?

It was probably good.

So I took a bite.

I left off the ice cream, though. Just in case.

I didn't think ice cream on meat pie would go.

"Oh," I said out loud.

"What?" Bubba asked.

He'd just come back.

"It's *pear* pie," I said.

Now I regretted leaving off the ice cream.

By the end? I'd most likely have more ice cream than pie.

Money for Nothing

I hate when that happened.

Well, not "hate." Hate's a strong word.

For my next bite? I took a huge spoonful of ice cream.

I wanted the ice cream to catch up. To the pie.

So I had a mouthful of food. Could barely chew.

The ice cream was cold.

"I'd like you to meet Rosa," Bubba said.

I was trying not to get a brain freeze.

Was trying to chew. Without biting on the cold ice cream.

I must have looked ridiculous.

But the small pretty woman? She just stood there.

Waiting.

Waiting for me to chew my food.

I felt so foolish.

Hilda's pie did that to me.

As I tried to warm the ice cream with my mouth, I also tried to smile.

Wrong move.

My mouth cracked open.

And I think a piece of crust came out.

"Really enjoying that pie, are you?" Bubba said.

I was so embarrassed.

I put my hand in front of my mouth.

I tried to finish it up.

I think I swallowed a slice of pear. Whole. Without even chewing.

Then I started choking.

Oh, yes. That helped things.

I looked really cool now.

But worse? I grabbed my cup of coffee. To help with the choking.

Only problem? It was scalding hot.

So I burned my mouth.

It felt hotter than it should have been.

Maybe due to the cold ice cream.

I spit out the scalding coffee. Right back into the cup.

I guess it could have been worse.

I could have spit it on the woman named Rosa.

Money for Nothing

"Are you okay?" she asked.

Bubba handed me a napkin.

"You've got a little drool," he said.

He pointed to my chin.

"Right there," he said.

I touched the napkin to my face.

Right where Bubba had pointed.

Nothing came off. The napkin was clean.

I looked at Bubba.

He was grinning.

"Very funny," I said. "I almost choke to death. And you're making fun of me."

He shrugged.

"Sorry," he said.

He didn't look sorry.

He turned to the young woman.

"Rosa? This is Dan. Dan Corbett. He just learned how to eat today. You'll have to excuse him."

He turned to me.

"Dan? This is Rosa. Rosa Cruz. We went to school together."

"We did not," Rosa said. "I was three years ahead of you."

Bubba turned back to Rosa. "I don't know why you always say that."

Rosa smiled. "Because it's true. When you were in ninth grade? I was in twelfth grade."

Bubba turned back to me. "I was a freshman. She was a senior. We were passionately in love."

"I barely noticed him," Rosa said.

"Okay. So *I* was in love," Bubba said.

Bubba was grinning.

"Look at her. Can you blame me?" Bubba asked me.

I *had* noticed how pretty she was.

I'd also noticed her smile.

When she smiled? The room lit up.

The sun seemed to shine a little brighter.

And my heart skipped a beat.

But maybe that was from choking.

Or the pie.

Or the scalding coffee.

Or my embarrassment.

Chapter 6

Just then, Henry came over.

Henry Pake. The town librarian.

"So how are you doing?" he asked me.

"Good," I said. "And you?"

"Good," he said. "Did you ever find out about those plans?"

"What plans?" Rosa asked.

Henry seemed as if he'd just noticed Rosa.

That was odd.

She'd been standing right next to him.

Guess he was so big and she was so small, he didn't see her.

He really was a big guy.

He had on a suit. But had his leather jacket over

it.

Guess he rode his bike here. His Harley.

He was bald. So you couldn't see if he had helmet head. You know. The dents in your hair? When you wear a helmet? That's called helmet head.

But you can't get it if you're bald.

"Oh. Hey, Rosa," he said. "Welcome home."

"Thanks," she said.

Then she smiled that high-beam smile of hers.

She was Latino. And had beautiful dark skin. So her smile looked even whiter.

But it was pretty white to begin with.

She had a great smile.

Did I already say that? Well, she did.

"What plans?" she asked again.

Henry looked at me.

I guess he didn't know if he should speak about it or not.

"It's okay," I told him. "They weren't top secret. Well, not to us, at least. They *were* to the men and women in Iraq. But not here."

Money for Nothing

"Now I *really* want to know," Rosa said with a grin.

"It's no big deal," I said.

"Yes it is," Bubba said.

Everyone was looking at me.

Well, not *everyone*. But everyone in our small group. Bubba, Rosa and Henry.

"Bubba found some plans. In a door. They were in one of my cars. In the junkyard."

"Oh," Rosa said. "So you're the guy. I'd heard that someone bought the junkyard from Dan."

"Yes," I said. "That's me."

"And *your* name is Dan," she noted.

I grinned. "I know. It's like… fate."

She giggled. "That's kind of funny."

I smiled. A *huge* smile.

I probably looked like an idiot.

But I couldn't help myself.

When she giggled like that? I just *had* to smile.

I noticed Bubba and Henry were also smiling.

But not at Rosa.

And not at me.

They were smiling at each other.

I didn't know what *that* was all about. But I didn't have time to think about it.

Rosa was asking me another question.

"So what about these plans?" she asked.

"It was really a map," I explained. "Of Iraq."

"Why was it in the guy's truck?" Henry asked.

"He was hiding it there. Hiding it until he went back," I said.

"What was the star?" Henry asked.

"The star?" Rosa asked.

She looked up at me. And I have to tell you. Those big brown eyes? They were amazing.

"It marked his source," I told them. I started to explain what a source was. But they stopped me.

"I know what a source is," Henry said. "They were lucky to have one over there."

I looked at Rosa. "I know what a source is as well."

Then everyone laughed. I didn't get the joke.

"The source was a boy," I explained. "So Mike bought the boy a personal DVD player. And some movies."

"Who's Mike?" Rosa asked.

"The man who died in the crash. The man who owned the truck," I told her.

"Oh," she said and nodded.

"And Dan here bought the kid a video game player. And a bunch of video games," Bubba said out loud.

I don't know why he'd said that. No one needed to know that.

"Did you get the stuff to the boy?" Henry asked.

I nodded. "Through a friend of Bubba's. Ramon. He got shipped out again."

Henry nodded. Then he smiled.

"I bet that kid won't know what hit him!" Rosa said.

"He deserves more than that," Henry said. "He put his life on the line. To help our people."

I agreed with Henry.

So did Rosa.

Then she turned to Henry.

"I thought you were talking about plans for another ballet," she said to Henry.

Ballet?!

I looked at Henry.

As he described himself: he's a big, bald tough-looking black man.

Ballet?

I knew he knit. But *ballet*?!

Chapter 7

"I'm sorry about your father," Henry said to Rosa.

Her father?

"We lost a great man when we lost him," Henry added.

Then it hit me.

"Jose was your *father*?" I croaked out.

Now I *really* felt embarrassed.

She nodded.

"I'm sorry," I said. "I shouldn't be here. I wasn't invited."

Rosa tilted her head.

"Everyone's invited," she said. "It's a funeral."

I still didn't get it. But maybe it'll take time.

"I heard that your father was a good man," I said softly.

She nodded. "He was."

"What did he do?" I asked. "You know, for a living."

She smiled. "It wasn't much of a living," she said with a short laugh. "But he loved what he did. He had a saying. 'I am rich although I am poor.'"

I was surprised. "Your father was poor?" I asked.

I had the idea that he was somewhat wealthy.

She smiled at that. And again, I was thrown off a little.

Her smile was dazzling. I wondered if it dazzled everyone. Or if it only dazzled me.

"Yes," she said. "But his students made him feel rich."

"He was a teacher?" I asked.

"Of sorts," she said. "He taught people how to read."

I nodded.

"He helped older people. People who were

learning English as a second language. People who never did quite learn how to read when they were younger," she explained.

"Like me," Bubba said with a grin.

I didn't know if he was fooling around. I couldn't tell sometimes.

"I figured I'd leave school when I was in ninth grade," he said with a grimace. "Thought I was all that."

Rosa laughed.

"But then I wanted to go for my GED," Bubba explained. "And I found out… I couldn't read."

I looked at Bubba.

He seemed to be telling the truth.

Then I looked at Rosa. Just to check.

Rosa nodded.

"No wonder you wanted to quit school," I told Bubba gently.

Bubba shrugged.

"School must have been very hard for you," I noted.

Bubba shrugged again.

"You had Brian in third grade. Right?" Rosa asked Bubba.

Bubba nodded.

"She was a *terrible* teacher!" Rosa said.

She was getting herself all worked up.

"My father couldn't *stand* that woman!" Rosa spit out. "He had more students that were in her class than all the other teachers put together!"

"Why was that?" I asked Rosa.

"Because she couldn't teach!" Rosa and Bubba said together.

"She'd destroy them in third grade," Rosa started.

"She had this way of humiliating kids," Bubba added.

"Then they'd eventually quit school," Rosa said.

"Like me," Bubba added.

"And she had this way of making kids feel like it was *their* fault. You know. That *they* couldn't learn," Rosa said with anger.

I looked at Bubba.

Money for Nothing

He nodded. "I now know that it was *her* fault," he said. "Dr. Brian's. Not mine."

"She had a *doctorate*?" I asked. I was shocked.

That made Bubba and Rosa laugh.

"*That's* why she thought she was so great," Bubba said.

"And why she stuck with her methods," Rosa added.

"Even though they didn't work? She thought she knew it all!" Bubba said.

Rosa sighed loudly.

"She was quite dangerous," Rosa said.

Then she shook her head.

"My dad counted the days until her retirement."

"When did she retire?" I asked.

Rosa snorted. "Until the day he died? He was *still* counting. She hung on."

"So she's *still* teaching?" I asked, horrified.

"If you can call it that," Bubba cracked.

"Is *she* why you left school? I asked him.

"I told people I left because Rosa here wouldn't give me the time of day."

Rosa smiled at Bubba. "Yeah, right," she said.

"For *real*," he teased.

She winked at Bubba. Then her smile widened.

It made me wish she were smiling at me.

"Anyhow, Jose taught me to read," Bubba said proudly. "It was then that the world opened up for me."

I nodded.

Bubba snorted. "I can't believe how stupid I was when I was a kid."

I shrugged. "You didn't know."

Then he laughed. "You can say that again. I didn't know a lot of things."

Rosa giggled. "Like how I wasn't interested in you."

"Well, *that*," he said with a chuckle. "But also how hard life can be. Especially if you don't have an education."

Henry agreed. "But you changed all that," Henry said to Bubba.

"Sure did," Bubba said with pride. "Thanks to Jose."

Chapter 8

"So where's Mel?" Rosa asked Henry.

Mel? I wondered who he was.

"At work. As usual." Henry rolled his eyes.

Rosa laughed. "Must be tough for you."

Henry made a face. "I manage."

I had no idea what they were talking about. Or who Mel was.

"Mel's Henry's partner in crime," Bubba said with a laugh.

Oh. His partner in crime. I think I understood now.

Okay. Whatever. Live and let live, and all of that.

I figured, who am I to judge another?

If that's what Henry wanted? Who was *I* to judge *him*?

I mean. Look at *my* life.

It sure wasn't anything special.

But this *may* shed some light.

I mean, really. Knitting?

Little pink dog sweaters?

And *ballet*?

That reminded me.

"So you do ballet?" I asked Henry.

If Henry were a dog? His fur would've just gone up.

You know. The fur at the back of a dog? When he's angry? And ready for a fight?

Henry's eyes got hard. Cold.

"You have a problem with that?" he said roughly.

His tone of voice said it all.

The man looked like he wanted to kill me. Snap me in two. Like a twig.

I held up my hands. "Whoa. No. No. No," I said. "I was just asking."

Money for Nothing

"How *did* you go from football to ballet?" Bubba asked with a grin.

I think Henry blushed. It was hard to tell.

His skin was quite dark.

But, yes. I think he was blushing.

His anger was gone.

Now he was embarrassed.

"Old Mrs. Hornsby wanted to do Swan Lake," he replied.

Bubba and Rosa laughed.

I didn't get the joke.

"I see," Bubba said. He jabbed his elbow at Henry.

Henry didn't look happy.

He didn't look *angry*. But he didn't look happy.

"I don't get it," I said.

"Mrs. Hornsby is on the town council," Rosa said. "Her money has helped get this town through many dry years."

"Still does," Henry said.

I still didn't get it.

"Her money built the new library," Bubba said.

Oh. It was starting to sink in.

I thought of the beautiful new building.

It sure must've cost a bit.

"So?" I said. "What does that have to do with you doing ballet?"

"Like I said. Mrs. Hornsby wanted to do Swan Lake," Henry repeated.

I shrugged.

I still didn't get it.

"She always wanted to be a ballet dancer," Henry said.

"And was she?" I asked.

"She weighs a good two fifty," Bubba said.

"More like three hundred," Henry said. "*I'm* two eighty."

I knew Henry had a problem with people making comments about his weight.

Turns out the kids were mean to him. At school. When he was a kid.

Now? I don't think *anyone* is mean to him.

"So what does that have to do with you?" I asked Henry.

Money for Nothing

"She wanted… to do… Swan *Lake*!" he said again. Like I was some sort of idiot or something.

"So?" I asked.

I *was* starting to feel like an idiot.

"How did that involve *you*?" I was trying to explain why I didn't get what everyone else seemed to get.

Or maybe I didn't want *Rosa* to think I was an idiot.

Rosa cracked up. So did Bubba.

Henry? He wasn't cracking up.

Chapter 9

Henry looked annoyed.

"I was the only one who could lift her, Dan!" he said.

"Ohhh," I said.

Now I got the joke.

"But after that first ballet?" he said. "I was hooked."

Bubba laughed.

"Hey," Henry said. "Knock it off!"

He was trying to look mean.

But his little smile? It belied his tone.

"It's harder then you'd think," Henry said. "A *lot* harder!"

Bubba snickered.

Money for Nothing

I said nothing.

"And it takes strength," Henry said. "*Great* strength."

Bubba was laughing loudly now.

The crowd at the diner? Still loud. But you could hear Bubba laughing. Over the noise.

"Takes strength? I'd guess it would," Bubba all but shouted. "If you're lifting up a three hundred pound woman!"

Henry didn't look amused. But he had a twinkle in his eye. So he wasn't annoyed, either.

"It takes discipline," Henry said. "Physical strength. Coordination. Not just brawn."

Bubba was still laughing.

I turned to Bubba. "I hear ballet takes great skill," I said.

"And grace," Bubba said. Then he started cracking up again.

Rosa stared at Bubba. "What's wrong with a man with grace?"

He shrugged. "I don't know."

Rosa made a face. "There's a *lot* you don't

know!" she told Bubba.

I liked Rosa.

She didn't take any grief from anyone.

She was small. But mighty.

I liked that about her.

Maybe Bubba brought it out. But I didn't think so.

It seemed she was *always* like that.

It was clear. She was a no-nonsense type of lady.

But not in a bad way.

In a good way.

And she had conviction. Beliefs.

She fought for what was right.

You could tell. She is a good person.

I wondered what she did for a living.

Just then, Rosa waived.

I followed her eyes. To see who she was waiving at.

My eyes bulged out.

I think I choked a little. On what? Who knew!

Maybe my own spit.

Money for Nothing

I stared at the woman Rosa was signaling.

Rosa was making hand gestures. They said, "Come here. Come here."

I watched. The woman came closer.

My mouth was hanging open.

Now, I must tell you. I come from New York.

I've *seen* beautiful women.

Patti was beautiful.

In New York? They're all over the place.

Everywhere you looked.

On Wall Street? It seemed there were many beautiful women.

They hung around the area.

Looking for rich men. Future husbands.

Like I said. They were everywhere.

Heck, in this *diner*? There were a few beautiful women.

Rosa was one of them. Probably the most beautiful in the diner.

But the woman Rosa was waving down?

I'd never seen a being like her in person.

Magazines? Yes.

Ads? Sure.

On TV? All the time.

But not in person.

And I *really* didn't expect to see someone like that… in Peaceville.

I watched as the woman opened the door to the diner.

I also saw just about every head snap in her direction.

Male *and* female.

This woman had a presence.

A real, physical presence.

I guess it's what Hollywood would call… star power.

Chapter 10

I watched as the woman strode over toward our little group.

I watched as the crowd split. To let her through.

I watched as a hush fell over the room.

I watched as she took long, elegant steps.

I watched as she flipped her head a little. And watched her hair fly into a perfect style. Like a TV ad.

I watched as she walked toward us.

She was getting closer.

Closer.

Closer still.

Then she walked up behind Henry. Leaned into him.

And kissed his big bald head.

Henry turned around.

Then he smiled.

"Hey, Rosa," the woman said. "I'm so sorry about your father."

I just stared. Stared at the creature before me.

She was so perfect. It was like she wasn't real.

"I'm sorry I'm late," she said to Rosa. "The shoot. It took longer than usual. The other model was a real pain."

"That's okay," Rosa said. "I understand."

"I had to do it," the woman said. "You know. Contracts and stuff."

"That's okay," Rosa said again.

"There are no clauses for funerals. Not for friends. Parents? Yes. Friends No."

"Stop worrying," Rosa said. "You're here now. That's all that matters, Mel."

Mel?! *This* was Mel?! This was *Mel*?!

Henry's… ah, *partner*?

This Mel was not *anything* like what I'd pictured.

Money for Nothing

I was shocked!

"This is your *partner*?" I said to Henry.

It just came out. I knew it wasn't polite. But it just came out.

Henry tugged the gorgeous woman to his side.

"My wife, really," Henry said.

My mouth went dry.

After what I'd pictured to be Henry's partner? This wasn't it. *She* wasn't it. It wasn't even a *she*!

"I didn't know you were married," I said to Henry.

He shrugged. His huge shoulders rose and fell. Like giant moving mountains.

Then it hit me.

"I was in your office. You don't have any pictures of your wife on your desk. Just your dog," I said.

Again he shrugged.

"It's a little crass of me to put her picture out," he said simply.

"Crass?" I asked.

That was a weird word to use.

Plus, if I had a wife that looked like her? I'd keep her picture on my desk.

I certainly kept plenty of Patti on my desk.

I loved looking at her picture. Especially when my day was rough.

"Yeah, crass," Henry said.

"Why?" I asked.

Bubba cracked up. Then he shook his head.

"She's a *super model*, Dan," Henry said.

"Yeah," Bubba said. "It would be like showing off. Bragging."

"No it wouldn't," I argued. "It would be *normal*. Like a man having a picture of his wife."

Henry thought about that.

"You know what? You're right, Dan," he said.

"Yes," I said. "I am."

"Why don't you put that one of Mel on the cover of Vogue? Last month's issue," Rosa said.

"That one was amazing," Bubba said.

"I *did* like that picture," Henry said.

He looked at his wife. Lovingly.

"I think I'll use that as the desktop photo. On

all the computers. At the library," Henry said.

He looked at me. "What do you think?"

I grinned. Crookedly. "That's kind of pushing it. Don't you think?" I asked.

He grinned right back.

"Now you see why I don't keep pictures of Mel at work," he said.

Yes. I guess I did.

"The teenage boys would love it," Bubba said.

"Yes," Henry said. "That might get them *in* to the library."

"You want teenage boys in the library? Use Mel's swimsuit edition picture," Bubba said.

He laughed loudly.

"Put it on all the computers," he cracked. "That'll get 'em breaking down the *doors* to come in."

"Right," Henry said. "That's just what I want."

They all laughed.

This town sure was wild.

Who'd ever guess? Our big, biker-dude librarian? He's married to a super model?!

Chapter 11

We moved on to the funeral after that.

It was sad. But not somber.

Many people spoke.

They all said the same thing.

Each in his own way.

"Jose was a good man," was heard throughout the ceremony.

One man was very touching.

"I am a migrant worker," he said. "My father was a migrant worker. *His* father was a migrant worker. None of us could read."

A tear slipped down this man's cheek.

I felt my own eyes start to water.

"Jose taught me to read," he said simply. "Then

Money for Nothing

he taught my father how to read."

"We are now American citizens," the man said.

"We owe that all to Jose."

The crowd thundered with applause.

"We could not take the test before. Because we could not read. Now we can read. Now we are citizens."

The crowd went nuts.

Cheering. Applauding. Whistling.

I was too.

Miles and Bubba were right.

Jose was a rich man. A man who had great wealth.

Love. Compassion. Empathy.

Jose had it all.

And he gave it all freely.

He gave people power.

He gave people strength.

He gave people a voice.

We heard from many people. All telling stories of success.

All because of Jose. Jose Cruz.

Then it was Rosa's turn to speak.

"Yes," she said. "My father was a good man. He cared about people."

She looked out at the huge crowd.

"He was a man of honor."

There was a hum of agreement. Then the crowd went silent.

"He made me love books. Through his passion."

Again, there was a hum of agreement.

"Although Dad liked science fiction," she said.

Then she chuckled.

"Me? I liked crime novels. Still do."

The crowd laughed.

I didn't know what was so funny.

But now was not the time to ask.

"I'd like to read for you now," Rosa said.

She took out a book.

It was well worn. Well read.

"This was my father's favorite book," she said.

The crowd chuckled.

I guess everyone knew Jose's favorite book.

Money for Nothing

"You may have heard it," she said.

The audience laughed again.

"I'd like to read from a short story."

She looked up from the book.

"Stop me if you've heard it already."

Again, the crowd chuckled.

I had no idea why.

"This passage is from a science fiction writer," she said.

"Isaac Asimov," the crowd called out.

Rosa smiled. "Right. It's from a story about a robot. A robot who wanted to be a human."

The crowd quieted.

She read a passage.

I remembered reading it. When I was younger.

It was a classic.

Not in the Shakespeare way.

But in the "must read" way.

"This was the first thing I remember Dad reading to me."

The crowd laughed again.

Jose must have read it to them, as well.

Elise Leonard

"His interest in words and books got me interested in words and books."

The crowd applauded.

"Dad's love was transferred through his work."

Another round of applause.

"Where else have you met someone as devoted?" she asked the crowd.

The crowd went wild.

"I'd like to read the three laws of robotics now," Rosa said.

She had a screen and a projector.

The words were up on the screen.

As she read, the crowd read along.

It was a testament to Jose's work.

The fact that everyone there could read those words.

> 1. A robot may not injure a human being or, through inaction, allow a human being to come to harm.
>
> 2. A robot must obey orders given to it by human beings, except where such orders would conflict with the First Law.
>
> 3. A robot must protect its own existence as long as such protection does not conflict with the First or Second Law.

Chapter 12

Rosa's reading of Isaac Asimov's Three Laws of Robotics[1] was great.

It must have been special to Jose. To everyone.

I know I enjoyed hearing them.

Her reading brought back good memories.

Memories of getting lost in a great story.

* * *

After the funeral? We all went back to the diner.

I hung out with Miles, Bubba, Henry and Mel.

---

[1] Isaac Asimov first introduced the Three Laws of Robotics in his 1942 short story "Runaround." It was later published in a book of short stories, entitled *I, Robot* (1950). "Runaround" was also printed in *The Complete Robot* (1982) and *Robot Visions* (1990).
Isaac Asimov, *I, Robot*, New York: Doubleday & Company, 1950.

Rosa was busy.

She was speaking with everyone.

"She's amazing. Isn't she?" Mel asked me.

I looked at Mel.

I was getting used to her stunning beauty.

At least a little bit. Enough to answer her. *Without* choking on my spit.

"Who's amazing?" I asked.

Bubba, Henry and Miles cracked up.

"You haven't taken your eyes off her," Mel said.

"Off who?" I asked.

Bubba snorted. "Are you *that* dumb, man? Or are you just playing dumb."

I should've taken offense. But I didn't.

I grinned.

I was busted.

I had to admit it.

"Just playing dumb," I said.

They all nodded. Mel included.

"You know," I said. "She just lost her father. She's *got* to be grieving. They seemed close."

Money for Nothing

"They were. Very," Mel said.

"But she's going around. Making everyone *else* feel better. You know. About her father's death."

It really amazed me.

No theatrics. No attention for herself.

She must have been in great pain.

But she was helping others.

"As I said," Mel repeated. "She's amazing."

"It seems she is," I replied.

Bubba held his hand out to Miles.

Miles slapped it.

"I'm not paying *you*," Miles said to Bubba.

Bubba looked shocked. "But you *owe* me!"

Miles shook his head.

"No way!" Miles said "You can't just *say* any old thing and think it's a bet."

Bubba pretended to be angry.

"*I* said that I bet you fifty bucks that Dan falls for Rosa," Bubba sputtered.

"Yeah, so?" Miles said. "I didn't *take* that bet. Anyone can *see* he likes the girl!"

I sat there staring at my two new friends.

"You *do* know I can hear you both. Right?" I asked them.

Bubba waved off my comment. "He owes me fifty bucks!" he whined.

Miles shook his head and rolled his eyes.

Then he smiled.

"I'll bet you fifty bucks that Hilda's coming with our food."

When Miles said that? Hilda was right behind Bubba.

When she placed the food over Bubba's shoulder? He cursed.

"There," Miles said. "Now we're even."

"Even?" Hilda asked. "About what?"

"Bubba's betting on stupid stuff again. Stuff *anyone* can see," Miles said to Hilda.

"I *don't* like Rosa!" I shouted.

Then I realized I must've come off sounding weird. And mean.

"Well, I *like* Rosa. I just don't *like* like Rosa," I said.

Henry laughed.

Money for Nothing

"What are we? Back in grade school?" he asked.

Mel hit Henry on his broad chest.

I could hear the hard thud. All the way over here.

The man must be one giant muscle.

I may not get it. Or why he does it. But that ballet stuff must be working.

"Knock it off, my husband," Mel said to Henry. "I think it's cute."

Hilda was busy putting everyone's plate before them.

"Is it—?" Mel started to ask Hilda.

Hilda cut Mel off. She looked insulted.

"Yes, Mel. It's organic. Don't even bother asking."

"Good. Good," Mel said.

"Would I give you anything else?" Hilda asked Mel. "I *know* what you like."

"Speaking of amazing," I said to Mel. "I think Hilda's amazing."

Chapter 13

"She knows what everyone in this town likes," I pointed out.

"Yes I do, Dan," Hilda said. "And I know you like Rosa. So stop being difficult."

I had to laugh.

"I meant that you know what everyone likes to *eat*," I explained.

"I know a lot more than *that*, sonny," Hilda said. "So behave."

Again. I had to laugh.

"And stop trying to change the subject. *No* one's going to fall for that move!" Hilda huffed.

Then she bustled off.

Mel picked up where she left off.

Money for Nothing

"Want to know about her?" she asked me.

I did. But I didn't want Bubba and Miles to know.

They'd bust my chops.

They'd show no mercy.

Well, Bubba would. Miles? Maybe not so much.

I didn't reply.

"I'll take that as a yes," Mel said.

Henry laughed.

"How can you take that as a yes?" he asked his wife.

She shrugged. "He didn't say no."

Henry reached over a tussled her hair.

Mel grinned at her husband.

It was funny seeing a super model with messed-up hair.

But then she shook her head. Like a wet dog does. And it was all back in place.

How did she *do* that?

Mel turned back to me.

"She left Peaceville. To go to college," Mel

began.

I listened closely.

"She wanted to explore the big city. Wanted to spread her wings. Be independent."

I could tell that about Rosa.

She seemed very independent.

I liked that about her.

"She studied law. Wanted to make a difference. Help others," Mel said.

"When we were kids? She was smart. Always had her nose in a book," Bubba said. "Those crime dramas. Detective stories. Stuff like that."

Mel nodded.

"She still does," Mel said with a laugh.

"So she's a lawyer now?" I asked.

"Yes," Mel said.

"Jose was really proud of her," Bubba said. "Bragged constantly."

"But he missed her," Miles said. "She lives so far away."

For some reason? My heart skipped a beat with those last words.

Money for Nothing

She lives so far away.

I guess it was best that way.

I wasn't ready to start a new relationship.

Not yet.

I wasn't even divorced from Patti yet.

She hadn't started the paperwork.

Perhaps she was keeping her options open.

Not that I'd take her back so quickly.

I don't even know if I'd take her back at all. My life was so different now.

I *liked* it the way it was now. Well, it *could* be a little more peaceful.

I mean, every car *did* seem to have a problem!

But I was handling the problems okay.

Sure, I wished I didn't *have* the problems. But how many more problems could there be?

My life would slow down sooner or later. Right?

I was thinking those thoughts when Rosa came to the table.

Chapter 14

All of a sudden? Everyone started to leave.

"Sorry. We've got to go," Mel said to Rosa.

"We do?" Henry asked.

Mel smacked Henry on the chest again. "Yes." She turned her head toward her husband.

She must have made a face or something.

Because Henry said, "Oh. Right. That's right. We've got to go. We've got that… thing… we have to do."

Mel rolled her eyes. "Smooth, dear. Really smooth."

They got up and left.

Miles cleared his throat. "I've got to go, too. Please excuse me."

Money for Nothing

Bubba pointed to the door. "I've got that, um, thing as well."

And he took off.

They left so fast? I was staring blankly at the door.

"What am I? A leper?" Rosa asked.

I turned toward Rosa.

I felt sorry for her.

Here, her father just died. And everyone is deserting her.

"I don't think it's you," I told her. "It's me."

Rosa giggled.

Her laughter tinkled.

It sounded like good wine glasses. When you clinked them together.

It was nice.

She sat there smiling at me.

I got a little nervous.

"So I hear you're a lawyer," I said.

"That's right."

Her hair was shiny. The sunlight was bouncing off it. Sending tiny starbursts every which way.

Her hair was dark. Not like Patti's blond hair.

But Rosa's hair seemed healthier. More… robust.

It had more luster.

I know this will sound stupid. But it seemed… honest.

It fit Rosa well.

She was just like her hair.

Shiny. Healthy. Honest.

"Do you like being a lawyer?" I asked her.

She smiled sadly.

"Don't tell anyone," she said softly. "But I've been telling people I love it."

I waited. There must be more to that sentence.

"But I don't."

That surprised me.

"Why not?" I asked.

"Well," she said. "I studied law to help people."

"And aren't you helping people?" I asked.

"I'm helping *some* people. But not the people I *want* to help."

Money for Nothing

Again, I waited.

"It's expensive to live in a city," she explained. "And I had to take a job that paid me well."

"You're lucky," I said. "You had that option. Many people don't."

She nodded. "Yes, that's true. But I'm really not that happy there."

"In the city? Or in the law firm?" I asked.

"Mostly the law firm," she said.

So. She liked living in the city. Far away from Peaceville.

That sort of hurt a little. Although I knew I shouldn't feel that way.

"Why?" I asked her. "Why don't you like the law firm?"

"I've seen too much," she said. "My ideals? They're shattered."

I looked at her. "I don't understand."

"Well," she started off slowly. "The rich? They get the better lawyers. Our system is not fair."

I thought about that.

"And big business?" she went on. "It's ruining

this country!"

She had a point there.

I could easily agree with her on that. "It's sad," I said.

"But true," she said quickly.

"Yes."

"I wanted to help people. Be like those lawyers on TV. Save my wronged clients. Prove who the real bad guys were."

She was so passionate.

It was hard not to admire her.

"And did you do that?"

She scoffed. "Hardly."

She looked so sad.

"I made some rich guys richer. That was all I did."

She looked even sadder.

"Or. As I should say. That's all I *do*," she added.

"What would you *like* to do? You know. With your life?" I asked her.

"Solve things. Help people. Bring justice," she

said.

"That's a tall order," I said.

She smiled.

"Is that a height crack? Because I may not be tall, but I'm—"

I held up my hands. "Whoa. No. It's not a crack at all. It's just a comment."

"Oh," she said softly. "Maybe I overreacted a bit. I'm a little sensitive about my height."

That made me laugh.

"We're all sensitive about *something*," I said.

She nodded.

"Did you know Henry is sensitive about his weight?" I asked her.

She nodded again. "The kids were really mean to him in school."

"Right," I said.

I looked at Rosa. Head on.

"There's nothing wrong with Henry's weight. It's perfect for his build. And there's nothing wrong with your height. It suits you perfectly."

She beamed. "Thanks, Dan."

Chapter 15

Just then my cell phone rang. "Hello?"

"Hey, Dan. It's me. Bubba."

I should have known.

"Is Rosa still there?" he asked.

I looked at Rosa.

"Yes. Why?"

"Tell her about the bag of money," he said.

I could hear Miles in the background. "Is he going to tell her about the money?"

"I just told him to tell her about it!" Bubba shouted back at Miles.

Then he hung up.

That was it.

The whole phone call.

Money for Nothing

I closed my phone.

"What bag of money?" Rosa asked.

"You heard that?" I asked.

She smiled sweetly. "It was hard not to."

Since she could hear? I was glad Bubba didn't say anything else. Anything that could have embarrassed me.

And we *all* know that Bubba would be the first to do *that* to me.

"Bubba found a bag of money," I told her.

"Where?" she asked.

"It was stuffed in an old Ford Torino."

"What year?" she asked.

"If I knew what *year* it was stuffed in there? I'd know *why* it was stuffed in there," I said with a grin.

"No," she said. "What year is the Torino?"

"Oh. 1971."

She nodded.

"I'm not going home for a few more days," she said. "Let's see if we can solve this crime."

"You think it's a crime?" I asked.

She smiled. "Who knows? I just like thinking that it is."

I smiled back.

If she wanted to solve a crime? That was fine with me.

I was just glad I could give her one to solve.

"Okay," I said. "Where do you want to start?"

"Can we start tomorrow?" she asked. "I've had a bit of a long day today."

Wow. It hit me. She'd just buried her father!

"I'm so sorry, Rosa," I said. "I was enjoying our chat so much. I forgot about… today."

She smiled warmly.

"For a little while? I did too," she said. "And please don't apologize. I want to thank you for that."

"Maybe you should not bother with this bag of money thing," I offered.

"No," she said. "Please. It's just what the doctor ordered. It'll be good not to think about Dad for a while. Plus, he'd want me to do this."

Chapter 16

The next day came quickly.

The sun was shining brightly.

We'd agreed to meet at ten o'clock. At the junkyard. In the morning.

I was a little nervous.

I don't know why.

It was 9:47AM. I was looking forward to seeing Rosa again. But like I said. I was a little nervous.

Miles came through the office door.

"Good morning," he said brightly.

"Rosa's coming," I blurted out.

Miles smiled deeply. "Well that's good."

His voice was deep. Solid. It was reassuring. It made me feel a little less nervous.

"I brought you this," he said.

He shoved an old stuffed animal at me.

"What's that for?" I asked.

"I thought you'd want it," he said.

I smiled. "It's been a while since I needed a stuffed animal," I said. "I sleep alone now."

Miles smiled.

"Good for you," he said. "I think."

He was grinning widely. His old face wrinkling up more than usual.

"I found it. Out there," he said.

His thumb hitched toward the northwest section of the yard.

"You can keep it," I told him.

He shook his head. "Oh, no. I don't want it."

"Then throw it out," I said.

He shook his head again. "I think it was that kid's stuffed animal. The one from years ago."

I had no idea what he was talking about.

"That kidnapped kid? On the news? About three years ago. You remember?" Miles asked.

I didn't remember. But now that he mentioned

Money for Nothing

it? It was coming back to me. A little. I think.

"Vaguely," I said.

"Well, before we throw it out? We should make sure. As far as I know? That kid was never found."

I sighed heavily.

I hadn't even started to figure out where that bag of money came from.

Now I had to solve a kidnapping?

Based on an old, dirty stuffed animal?

This was all too much.

"Look just don't tell Rosa about that stuffed animal. Okay?" I asked Miles.

"Sure thing, Dan."

"She's got enough on her mind. Her Dad. Now this bag of money thing. Just don't stress her out."

"I won't mention it," Miles said.

"Thanks," I said.

Just then the door opened.

And in walked sunshine itself.

Chapter 17

"You look great," I said.

She flushed a little. "I like yellow."

"You look great in it," I commented.

She blushed prettily. "Thanks."

"Well, I guess I should go," Miles said.

He hid the stuffed animal behind his back.

"Let me know if you need anything," he said to both of us.

"Okay," I told him.

"Will do," Rosa said. "Thanks, Miles."

Miles was almost out the door.

"Oh, and Miles?" Rosa said.

He turned back around to look at Rosa. The stuffed animal still hidden. "Yes?"

Money for Nothing

"It was really great seeing you a couple months back. I really enjoyed our lunch together. In the city. It felt good seeing someone from home."

So. Miles went to visit Rosa? He sure did get around when he wasn't here.

It made me wonder, yet again, where he went.

But, that wasn't my business.

"Me too," Miles said.

He nodded and left.

"So what do we do now?" I asked Rosa.

She sat in the seat in front of my desk.

"Let's see whose car it was, first."

I did a car facts report on the VIN. You know, the Vehicle ID number.

"Wow," I said. "I never would have guessed this!"

"What?" Rosa asked.

"The owner."

"Who was it?"

"It's showing an Agnes Hornsby," I said.

"That's Mrs. Hornsby."

"Why would *she* own a muscle car?" I asked.

"She has a son," Rosa replied. "His name's Archibald."

"Archibald Hornsby?" I said.

I shook my head and laughed.

"Who would do that to a child?!" I wondered.

"I know," Rosa said. "And what's worse? He was the *third*."

I said it out loud. "Archibald Hornsby the third."

Rosa chuckled. "We called him Archie."

"Good thinking."

Rosa nodded. "He was really very nice."

I laughed. "I guess you'd have to be. With a name like that."

"I know. It sounds stuffy. But *he* isn't."

"Where can we reach him? Where does he work?" I asked her. "Do you know?"

She grinned. "Yup. But you're not going to believe it."

"Try me."

"He's a congressman."

It figures.

Chapter 18

We put in a call.

His secretary answered.

"I'm sorry," she said. "He's tied up right now."

Rosa talked loudly so the lady could hear. "Tell him Rosa Cruz is calling. Tell him it's personal."

Within seconds, a man picked up the phone.

"Rosa? How *are* you! I was sorry to hear about your dad. Sorry I couldn't make it to the funeral."

"It's not Rosa. But she's here," I said.

"Hi, Archie," she called out.

"Tell her I said hello," the man said.

"He says hello," I told Rosa. "And he's sorry to hear about your father. And that he couldn't make it to the funeral."

Rosa nodded.

"Don't worry," she said. "I understand."

"Good. Good," he said. "Now. With whom am I speaking?"

I had to smile. He *did* sound a little stuffy to me.

"Dan," I said. "Dan Corbett."

"Oh," he said. "Right. You now own the junkyard."

Wow. He was really in the know.

As if he read my mind, he spoke. "I have to keep up on things. I tend to be able to keep many facts in my head at once."

I was impressed.

"Well, then maybe you'd remember a '71 Ford Torino?"

He chuckled. "I remember it well."

"Any chance you remember a bag of money in it?" I asked him.

"Sure do," he replied.

Great. A congressman. A bag of money. This didn't sound good.

Money for Nothing

I didn't know if he was going to tell me about it.

He sure wasn't volunteering any info.

"Was it *your* money?" I asked.

"No. The money was my mother's," he finally said.

Then he stopped talking.

"Anything else?" I asked.

He sighed. "Oh, okay," he said. "She was squirreling it away. Giving me money here and there. While my dad was alive."

That didn't seem so bad.

"My dad was a real tightwad. He still had the first nickel he ever made. He sold lemonade at a stand. When he was 8!"

Again, that didn't seem so bad.

"It embarrassed my mother. A *lot*. She's quite generous. And he didn't even give her enough for groceries. Yet, he was greatly wealthy. My home life was not what people thought."

Rosa leaned toward me. Or the phone.

"I guess not," she said loudly.

Obviously, she could hear him speaking.

"When my father died? She got all his money. The old stingy coot's money was finally used for some good," he said.

He laughed. It was hallow.

"I forgot about that bag of money. But it's my mother's. You'll have to ask her what she wants to do with it."

I looked at Rosa.

She nodded.

"Thanks, Archie," she called to the phone.

"No problem, Rosa."

"Yes," I said. "Thank you."

"My pleasure, Dan. If I can ever be of help to you? Please let me know."

Again, I was impressed with him.

"Thank you," I said.

I hung up.

"Let's call Mrs. Hornsby," Rosa said.

Chapter 19

I let Rosa make this next call.

We traded chairs.

She looked cute in my desk chair.

She got lost in it.

It was so much larger than she was.

"Hi," she said. "Mrs. Hornsby? It's Rosa. Rosa Cruz."

Rosa smiled at me. Then she winked.

I winked back.

"Yes. Thank you. I'm fine," Rosa said.

She listened.

"I miss him too. Thank you," she said. "I'm calling because I have a question to ask you. It's about a bag of money. From Archie's old Torino."

The woman must be quite a talker.

Rosa waited for Mrs. Hornsby to explain.

It took a long time!

But I waited.

I had no other choice.

"That will be perfect!" Rosa finally said.

Then she hung up.

"That was it?" I asked Rosa.

"That was it," she said with a smile.

"What did she say?" I asked.

"She said to give the money to the library. In my father's name."

"It's a *lot* of money!" I said. "Is she sure?"

Rosa snorted a laugh. "It's *nothing* compared to what she has now. A drop in the bucket."

"So what now?" I asked her.

"Did you have breakfast yet?" she asked.

I didn't want to tell her. Tell her I was too nervous to eat this morning. Too nervous because *she* was coming over.

"No," was all I said.

"Let's call everyone and meet at the diner," she said.

Money for Nothing

"Good idea," I said.

We called everyone up.

They all said they could meet at the diner in twenty minutes.

* * *

So there we were.

All at the diner.

Sitting around.

It was really very nice.

Who was there?

Hilda, of course.

And Bubba, Miles, Henry, Mel and Rosa.

"She wants you to buy a bunch of books and CDs for the library," Rosa told Henry. "In honor and in memory of my father."

Henry was excited.

"I'll buy a few collections of everything from Isaac Asimov," Henry said. "And of course, I'll get a few of the movies *I, Robot* and *Bicentennial Man*."

"Of course," Rosa said with a grin.

"I feel badly for getting money for nothing," he

said. "Rosa should get that money."

"Why?" Rosa asked. "I don't deserve it. Sometimes? We all get money for nothing."

"I get money for standing around," Mel said.

I agreed with Rosa. "I get money for selling old, used cars and parts," I said.

Rosa punched my arm.

"It's called recycling, Dan!" she said. "You know. Recycle and reuse!"

Henry shrugged.

"I guess I can get money for loaning out books," he said.

"That's right," Rosa said. "Look at me. I get money for helping the rich get richer."

Miles groaned.

"Hey, I'm not *proud* of it. But it *is* money for nothing," Rosa chimed in.

"Am I the *only* one around here who works for his money?!" Bubba asked loudly.

Bubba had that devilish grin on his face. The one my old Aunt Sue would say showed that Bubba was up to no good.

Now that Dan has solved *this* problem, read the next **JUNKYARD DAN** book, **STUFFED ANIMAL**, to find out about that stuffed animal Miles found. Did it belong to the kidnapped boy? Or was it just some old stuffed animal? If it did belong to that boy, will Dan find the child? Is the boy even still *alive*? Find out by reading the *next* book in the series!

And we have a few **other** series that you might like too:

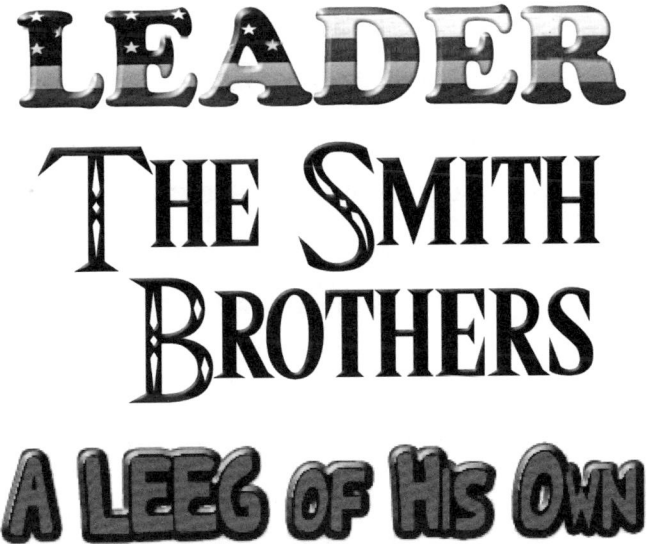

LEADER

THE SMITH BROTHERS

A LEEG OF HIS OWN

Want to read more NOX PRESS books?

Go online to
www.NoxPress.com
to see what's being released!

Books can easily be purchased online or you can contact **Nox Press** via the Website for quantity discounts.

Are you a fan?

Do you want us to put *your* comments up on our Website?
If so, please e-mail them to:
NoxPress@gmail.com

NOX PRESS
books for that extra kick to give you more power
www.NoxPress.com